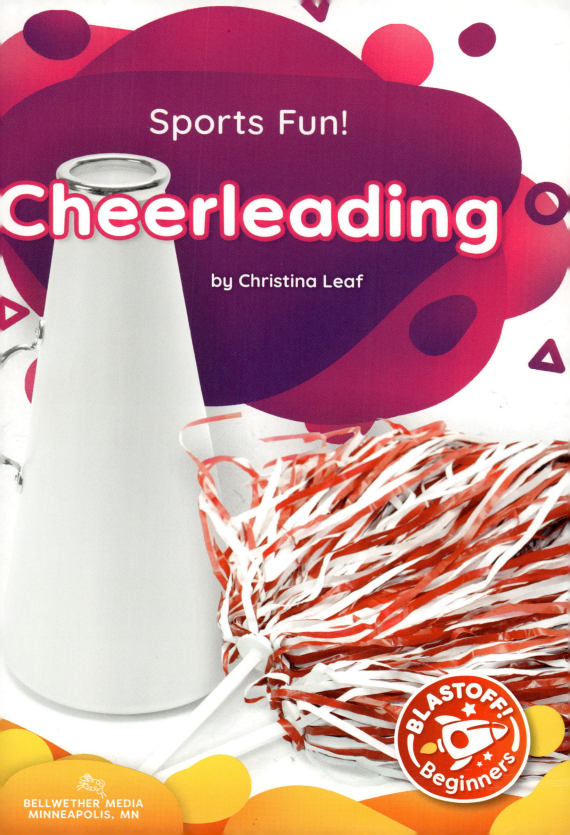

Blastoff! Beginners are developed by literacy experts and educators to meet the needs of early readers. These engaging informational texts support young children as they begin reading about their world. Through simple language and high frequency words paired with crisp, colorful photos, Blastoff! Beginners launch young readers into the universe of independent reading.

Sight Words in This Book

a	here	other	this
and	is	people	to
are	jump	she	up
did	many	some	use
do	may	the	
get	on	they	

This edition first published in 2024 by Bellwether Media, Inc.

No part of this publication may be reproduced in whole or in part without written permission of the publisher. For information regarding permission, write to Bellwether Media, Inc., Attention: Permissions Department, 6012 Blue Circle Drive, Minnetonka, MN 55343.

Library of Congress Cataloging-in-Publication Data

Names: Leaf, Christina, author.
Title: Cheerleading / by Christina Leaf.
Description: Minneapolis, MN : Bellwether Media, Inc., 2024. | Series: Blastoff beginners: Sports fun! | Includes bibliographical references and index. | Audience: Ages 4-7 | Audience: Grades K-1
Identifiers: LCCN 2023004970 (print) | LCCN 2023004971 (ebook) | ISBN 9798886873924 (library binding) | ISBN 9798886875805 (ebook)
Subjects: LCSH: Cheerleading--Juvenile literature. | Cheerleaders--Juvenile literature.
Classification: LCC LB3635 .L43 2024 (print) | LCC LB3635 (ebook) | DDC 791.6/4--dc23/eng/20230201
LC record available at https://lccn.loc.gov/2023004970
LC ebook record available at https://lccn.loc.gov/2023004971

Text copyright © 2024 by Bellwether Media, Inc. BLASTOFF! BEGINNERS and associated logos are trademarks and/or registered trademarks of Bellwether Media, Inc.

Editor: Rebecca Sabelko   Designer: Jeffrey Kollock

Printed in the United States of America, North Mankato, MN.

Table of Contents

Here to Cheer!	4
What Is Cheerleading?	6
Jumps and Tosses	10
Cheerleading Facts	22
Glossary	23
To Learn More	24
Index	24

Here to Cheer!

Cheerleaders smile and wave. They are here to cheer!

What Is Cheerleading?

Cheerleading is a team sport. Some teams cheer on other sports.

Some teams do **routines**. They try to get many points.

Jumps and Tosses

Teams wear **uniforms**. Many use **pom-poms**.

uniform

Teams yell.
They clap.
They hold signs.

sign

Teams dance to music. They do jumps!

jump

They do **stunts**.
She is up high!

Teams may toss people. She did a flip! Wow!

This team got the most points. They win!

Cheerleading Facts

Cheerleading

pom-pom

uniform

routine

Cheerleading Moves

dance

jump

do stunts

22

Glossary

pom-poms

fluffy balls of streamers

routines

sets of movements done in order by a team

stunts

cheerleading moves where people are lifted up

uniforms

clothes that everyone in a group wears

To Learn More

ON THE WEB

FACTSURFER

Factsurfer.com gives you a safe, fun way to find more information.

1. Go to www.factsurfer.com.

2. Enter "cheerleading" into the search box and click 🔍.

3. Select your book cover to see a list of related content.

Index

cheer, 4, 6
clap, 12
dance, 14
flip, 18
jumps, 14, 15
music, 14
points, 8, 20
pom-poms, 10, 11

routines, 8, 9
signs, 12
smile, 4
sports, 6
stunts, 16, 17
team, 6, 8, 10, 12, 14, 18, 20
toss, 18, 19
uniforms, 10

wave, 4
win, 20
yell, 12

The images in this book are reproduced through the courtesy of: Mega Pixel, front cover; Danny E Hooks, front cover; Wira SHK, p. 3; Tetra Images/ Alamy, p. 4; Anton Vierietin, p. 5; JoeSAPhotos, p. 7; linkpusher, pp. 9, 17, 22 (stunt); William Perugini, pp. 10 (uniform), 23 (uniforms); North Charleston/ Flickr, p. 11; DNDavis, p. 12 (sign); Aspenphoto, p. 13; Cherednychenko Ihor, pp. 15, 19, 22 (cheerleading, dance, jump), 23 (routines); Pavel L Photo and Video, pp. 21, 23 (stunts); WoodysPhotos, p. 23 (pom-poms).

24